Born of Serbian heritage and raised in Kazakhstan, Austria, and Switzerland, Barbara Matijevic has integrated her multicultural upbringing into her writing that is not apparent in retrospect, but is rather a delicate whisper in the wind—a sensation that lingers within the unspoken spaces between the lines.

Barbara's profound affinity for the sea is a cornerstone of her life, having grown up sailing the Mediterranean with her family. The sea's enigmas often seep into her writing, becoming a powerful metaphor for life's complexities.

Writing, her closest companion since childhood, developed with poetry and evolved into prose complemented by melodic undertones. Barbara's style of writing is poetic, resounding with the boundless sea. She relishes in developing novel narratives, analogous to plunging into uncharted waters, guiding her writing toward unseen horizons as a writer.

Barbara Matijevic

THE AEONIAN

AUSTIN MACAULEY PUBLISHERS™

LONDON • CAMBRIDGE • NEW YORK • SHARJAH

A CIP catalogue record for this title is available from the British Library.

ISBN 9781035850273 (Paperback)
ISBN 9781035850297 (ePub e-book)

Lucas

www.austinmacauley.com

First Published 2024
Austin Macauley Publishers Ltd®
1 Canada Square
Canary Wharf
London
E14 5AA

For Joan

Table of Contents

To all the words left unspoken
The regrets of choices unmade
The incessant echoes of what could have been

To all the chapters longed to be read,
Forced shut far too soon.

"Within every sane mind there was a trace of insanity, and within the depths of madness glimmered a seed of lucidity."

—Elif Shafak, 10 Minutes 38 Seconds in *This Strange World*

Preface

From the day my writing journey began, the dream of having a book under my name had been a constant flutter in my mind. Though I continued to devote myself to the written word, the stories I created never made it past the drafting stage. Unfinished manuscripts would gather dust, and for days or even months at a time, I would cease writing altogether.

However, as the final year of high school unfolded, something stirred within me and aboard the train to school, I devised a goal I pledged to fulfil: write and print out a book by the end of the school year. The seeds of what you now hold in your hands were planted at that moment, and I set out on the journey of writing my first novella. With no delay, upon entering my room, I conceived a story in my mind for which I began writing. Little did I know, how challenging it would be to see it through to completion.

Though procrastination was a major obstacle, the greatest one was doubt. Throughout the entire journey, *Doubt* sat beside me, relentlessly whispering that I was incompetent, that every word I put out was of no value, and that I was doing nothing but wasting my time. As much as I was able to dismiss it, there were moments when life hit me unexpectedly, leaving me prone to uncertainty. That was when *Doubt* dealt its hardest blows.

And yet, after enduring countless fights and bearing numerous blows, I overcame that seemingly insurmountable obstacle. How else would you be holding this book?

A story should never be read statically; it should be read with an open mind and inward eye. Each page offers its own interpretation and perspective, and it is my hope that this novella will speak to you in a personal and meaningful way. On its surface, the story is merely an exploration of desire and its ramifications, but in its depths, it encapsulates all of my innermost thoughts and feelings, spilled out onto these short pages.

Always

Some would say she was his nicotine
Alluring
Insidious
—Persistent—

He loved her just as much
As he hated her

~~Geraldine~~
A name to be known
A name never forgotten
The source of his utmost bliss
And unrelenting misery

But she was more than that
Something greater
Something more powerful
Something
—Divine—

In search of an angel in the skies,
He grasped within reach

A shadow
A hush
An unfathomable depth

Not dead
Nor alive

A ghost
A beating heart
An insatiable hunger

He sat
on the edge of the abyss,
waiting
—*Patiently*—

Casting a line
for his fallen light

Everyone holds a chapter
they refuse to recite

And yet
His unspoken chapter
~~*Geraldine*~~
Had been inscribed.

—*Immortalised*—By ink

Perpetually
—*Geraldine*—
Eternal

Geraldine
Always Present

Impulse

In the distance, thunder resounded as torrential rain fell, battering his warlock-black covert coat, all while soaking his fraying Oxford shoes. In front of him stood the entrance to a hotel tucked away deep within the Austrian Alps, its imposing brown facade dominating the landscape. He had been anticipating this moment for years. Preparation had gone into every interaction. Every outcome had been planned. Every occupant of the building—studied. Finally, it had reached the point of execution. All it took was a three-time pelt of the door knocker.

Even so, he hesitated.

Am I ready? Should I return a year from now?

What if I forgot something? What if everything doesn't go as planned?

It is with this shift in energy that hesitancy arose.

No, he thought, *I'm not ready.*

With that final intrusive thought, he turned to leave. A slow descent down the doorsteps followed, his coat pressed firmly against his body as he struggled against the cold. In a blink, the door swung open, revealing a woman standing at its threshold. In her stance, she did not reach further than the doorknob. An erect posture and tremulous arms underscored her frail complexion and dwindling vigour. A glare swept across her face. On the bridge of her nose sat golden specs that framed her piercing emerald eyes. In a pair of brown slacks, and slippers of white fur, her figure stood rigid, cloaked in a cotton coat so large it almost swallowed her up.

Hello, Margareta, he thought.

"Welcome to the Aeonian, how may I help you?" she said, posing a fake smile in place of her expressionless stare.

His expression softened as he replied, "I booked a room here for two nights. We spoke yesterday."

Behind the golden specs, her eyes grew, resembling those of a Tarsier. As a matter of fact, she and Tarsiers shared a lot in common: shy, introverted, and protective of their territory, patrolling regularly, pouncing on any intruder that posed a threat to their invaluable space.

"Graham Wagner?" she asked, her eyes wide with anticipation, not blinking or fluttering from his sight. He replied with a nod, retaining the smile on his face.

Glancing into his eyes, she studied him for a few seconds before turning and moving into the building as he followed behind. A lanky man with a stance well above two metres greeted him at the doorway, his appearance reminiscent of a Great Egret.

Adalrik, as Graham had expected.

The man's personality matched that of the animal as well—deceptively relaxed, yet capable of erupting in shrill, violent screams at the slightest provocation. Adalrik held his stance firm, not shifting gaze towards Graham as he extended his sinuous, slender arm before him.

"Coat," he said, his posture rigid. With his coat soaked through, Graham handed it over to the man, following shortly after Margareta who had already begun to advance deeper into the building. There was a predominant presence of walnut wood within the interior of the house, characterised by divergent ring patterns marked by a rich golden-brown hue. In the wood lines, dents, and colouration, distinct characteristics reflected the house's infirmity. Taking him along a narrow hallway, Margareta led him to a carved wood door at the end of the corridor. Two thin lines outlined the shape of the door's arch, embellished with three chiselled roses. Rust lined the outer edges of a circular doorknob that lay lower than usual. With fumbling hands, Margareta slowly turned the knob, it's worn exterior creaking as she opened the door. Graham watched the door open, filling the hallway with a warmth that sent chills down his spine. Upon entering the room, he was struck by its stark contrast to the hotel's claustrophobic entrance. The floor was a rich, warm tone of teak wood, adorned with plush rugs, a cosy couch set, and a diminutive coffee table. In the centre, a crackling fire danced away, casting a soft glow over the room.

It was then that he saw *her*.

Geraldine…

Lounging in a corner of the living room, she sat curled up in a grey plush blanket on an armchair, deeply absorbed in a book. Her brown, wavy hair was clipped into place, a few stray strands framing her face. Her delicate, pale blue eyes

shone behind her clear spectacles, radiating the warmth he
sorely missed.

In his eyes, she was *perfect*.
In her essence, she embodied *pure divinity.*

He missed her giggles and laughter late at night
as she lay, deeply absorbed in
a book -
The glint in her eyes whenever discussing topics
she was passionate
about -
The way her wavy, chestnut-coloured hair caressed
her delicate white complexion -
The pervasive smell of charred food in the kitchen, resulting
from her clumsiness
when cooking -
Her obsession with having the optimum blend of coffee
infused with
a slight hint of cinnamon and vanilla-

The smooth and delicate lips that graced both his morning
coffee
and evening slumber.

-He missed *her*-
-His heart ached for *her*-
-His soul yearned for *her*-
-His one and only —*desire*— was-
-Her-
-Her-
—Her—

In a moment of clarity, he recalled his need to adhere to the plan. Moving further into the space, he followed Margareta as she made her way to the right side of the room where a broad, irregular table stood. Tea, coffee, cookies, and other sweet snacks were presented on a white linen cloth embossed with bears and foxes. Dim light poured from candlesticks around the table, as drips of wax cascaded from their stems, coating the cloth in a mound of hardened wax. Just as he had expected, Margareta spoke, "There should be no more than one snack per person. I do not wish to catch you helping yourself to more than you need." He smiled and nodded in response.

With an accusatory look in her eye, a muttering escaped her lips as she bundled herself tightly into her arms. Amid the silence, she slowly turned and scuffled to the door, slamming it shut, eliciting a shrill sound that briefly broke the silence in the room. While all other occupants turned their attention to the door, visibly agitated, Geraldine remained absorbed in her book, seemingly unscathed. As Graham flicked on the switch of the kettle, he plucked an Earl Grey tea bag and cast a quick glance around the room, his gaze wandering about as he patiently awaited the water to reach boiling point. His gaze came to a halt at the two men seated on the couch by the withering fire. As with the hostess, the hotel's occupants were peculiar.

Herbert and Merdian

Seated across the crackling fire, the two sipped tea, each lost in conversation while casting occasional glances at the dancing flames. The room exuded an air of formality, both men attired in suits and ties with meticulously groomed hair. A pungent scent wafted about them, mingling with the fire's smoky aroma. Herbert sported a grey suit with a matching vest and black tie. A pair of sleek grey specs perched on the bridge of his nose, accentuating his enlarged eyes, reflecting the glimmering firelight. His unkempt eyebrows sprouted wildly above his face, a sharp contrast to his neatly coiffed hair. Merdian, his counterpart, donned an emerald suit with a black button-up shirt. His dirty blonde hair, slightly curly, was trimmed short on the sides and left long on top. In their outfits, there was one point of difference—soft blush-coloured slippers bearing the words "Aeonian".

Across from Geraldine —*her*— stood a chubby man and a petite, slender woman in the bottom left corner of the room. Immediately, he recognised them and their contradictory looks.

Herald and Caroline

It felt as if some aspects of their appearances had been stolen from each other, as their overall aesthetics did not correspond. Caroline possessed wavey, glacier-blonde hair, offset by a pair of warlock black eyes. Herald's sleek, inky hair juxtaposed a pair of light blue eyes. The tall, corpulent figure of his reduced the size of hers, making her appear petite and much slimmer than she was. In turn, she made him appear bulkier and more imposing. His slender frame and upright posture highlighted her slouched posture. His bushy eyebrows complimented her thin, well-kept ones. His overgrown, dirty fingernails—her short, well-kept acrylics. His drab, overworn jumpsuit—her refined, vibrant attire.

And yet, despite these contradictory highlights, in some strange way, they complemented each other's appearance. In their imperfection, they were the perfect couple.

Just then, Graham caught sight of a raven perched on the windowsill beside them. The opaque entity gazed at him intently from the inky depths of the night. In wake of the judgment that surged within his being, he felt compelled to retreat without delay and put an end to the whole affair. However, this notion was quickly cast aside as he shifted his gaze to the right side of the room where *she* was seated.

Geraldine…

His trance, broken by the click of the kettle, prompted him to turn back and pour the hot water into his mug. He watched as the once-clear water transformed into a *murky black*, its flavour slowly dispersing itself, taking over, forever changing the water into its own. Almost like a *disease,* it permeated the once-neutral condiment, leaving darkness in its place. Having removed the teabag, he propped it in a napkin, placing it in the adjacent container. In passing, he glanced at the milk pot beside the kettle. The notion of ruining such a drink with an overwhelming dose of sweetness and diluting its intensity with a universally bland ingredient such as milk perplexed him. The condiment was perfect *as it was.* Intense, keen and imposing—in its own right, it was unmatched. There was no need to add additional ingredients that permeated its individuality and transformed it into a drink like all others: sweet and neutral. It was all that it needed, as such, he preferred it. As he turned once more, firmly clutching the mug, he took a sip of the potent, bitter brew. It slithered delicately past his lips, blanketing his frigid core with an enveloping warmth. But as quickly as it came, the warmth receded, consumed by the indignity that resounded within him. He then approached the two gentlemen in the lounge and seated himself on the nearest armchair.

Tap. Tap.

His gaze flicked back to the window that stood beside Herald and Caroline. A sombre raven dwelt by the windowsill, malice, and decay permeating its being. As he caught its gaze, an unsettling current swept through him, draining the room of warmth.

Judgment prevailed.

All else in the room faded from his consciousness as he stood, caught in its trance. He despised surrendering control as it was all he ever craved. Breaking the gaze, he turned to the men and readied himself to speak.

Tap. Tap.
  Tap. Tap.

He looked back at the raven once more as it glared at him with intent. A warning. A judgment of what was to come. He knew the meaning behind its presence. He understood the purpose. He knew what had to be done. But there was one thing that would always convince him otherwise.

Geraldine…

He fixated upon its deep-set, predatory eyes, his heart unwavering as he held his gaze steady on the creature. Nothing could deter him from reaching his destination, and the beast knew it too. Abruptly, it ceased its pursuit and retreated into the forest, leaving in its wake an overwhelming sense of judgment. Calm and conviction flooded his being, he knew he could finally proceed with his plan, *untamed*.

Cough.

Herbert and Mardian turned to him, both exhibiting a look of surprise tempered with a hint of irritation. Promptly, he spoke before their annoyance turned to antagonism, "How's the Aeonian?"

Their eyes widened in confusion as they briefly glanced at one another. A shrug was exchanged, and both turned back to him as Mardian spoke, "It's quite alright…"

Silence engulfed the room. Graham sensed the growing tension and discomfort between them. Soon, Herbert spoke, "…how are you liking the Aeonian?"

Graham's lips curled into a smile as he responded,

"It's not what I'm used to."

He intentionally left it at that, and as the seconds ticked by, the tension between the two men grew more palpable. Abruptly, Herbert's voice broke the silence, "Well, to be exact, we're in the same boat here. I'm Herbert, and this fella next to me is Mardian. We just got in yesterday… the weather has been a mess. Not exactly what I had in mind for our trip, you know? But hey, maybe you're one of those folks who loves a good storm. No judgment here, of course. We all have our preferences. For us, though, it's just getting in the way of our plans. We've got things to do, places to go, errands to run. And with this weather, it's starting to feel like we'll never get to the Hedge. But like I said, to each their own. Maybe you're a big fan of the rain and wind. It's just that it's not practical for us, is all. And besides the point. "Herbert!" Mardian interrupted, his gaze fixed on Graham.

An awkward moment ensued once more, as both fell into silence. Nevertheless, Graham did not mind. He had found exactly what he was looking for. An informational slip. Suddenly, Mardian spoke, "What brought you here, Mr—"

"Graham Wagner," Graham intervened.

"Ah, what brings you here Mr. Wagner?" Mardian replied, his fingers fidgeting with the end of his tie. Graham sat there for a moment, his gaze shifting between the two of them. A brief smile played on his lips as he adjusted his slouched posture, "The same thing that brought *you* here."

Oblivion

They sat there, in utter silence, lost for words. In his demeanour, Herbert's face exuded sheer panic and confusion as he spoke up, "I don't know what you're talking about."

A trickle of sweat ran down Herbert's chubby cheeks. Graham adjusted his posture, folding back into the couch. He took a sip of tea from his mug, briefly looking out the window, before turning to face both men.

"Don't take me for an idiot."

Mardian grasped Herbert by the shoulder, clearly in a much calmer state than his younger brother. He turned to Graham and spoke in a measured tone, his breathing steady and his movements slow, "What do you want?"

Graham smiled, straightening the sleeves of his button-up shirt.

"As I said before, I'm here for the same thing as you." Mardian repositioned the golden specs that had strayed from his nose, seemingly untouched by Graham's confidence. Herbert had calmed himself to some degree but seemed to have given up on contributing to the conversation, devoting his attention to the dwindling flames in front of him. Again, Mardian spoke, "That's not what I asked. I am aware of where you want to go. I want to know what a man such as yourself is looking for here."

Graham had expected Mardian's composed demeanour in the face of stress. According to his research, the brothers had grown up in an abusive household and developed different coping mechanisms. Herbert had turned fragile and vulnerable, while Mardian developed a resolute and unyielding attitude. Mardian was always responsible for taking care of his younger siblings, including Herbert, who was spared some of the abuse but not all. Yet, despite Mardian's inherent tough skin, one thing always caused his walls to crumble with no effort.

The possibility of love

—driven—

by his fear of loneliness.

"Look to your left," Graham said.

Mardian turned around with a slow and audible exhale, his frustration palpable. Graham could tell the moment Mardian's eyes fixated on Geraldine. His stiff shoulders loosened up, and his once-crimson ears had returned to the natural pallor of his skin. After a brief pause, he turned his attention back to Graham.

"What about her?" he said, his hand toying with the tip of his tie.

"She likes you. I can see it in her eyes," Graham spoke softly.

Mardian's cheeks turned red as he turned back toward her once more. Geraldine had not noticed his observation, still engrossed in the book she read.

How can you be so…perfect? So…divine?

As Mardian turned back to face Graham, Graham spoke once more, "I'll make you two a deal. I know her. Our relationship goes back a long way. I can set up a date between you both, but I need something in return."

Graham looked towards Herald briefly before turning to speak to Mardian, "Your brother needs to take me there."

"Where?" Mardian replied.

Graham directly met his gaze and spoke once more, "The Hedge."

Silence permeated the room as they stared at one another.

Herald had not noticed the conversation and was still lost in thought, his eyes glued to the fireplace. Mardian's gaze lingered on Geraldine for a few moments longer, his eyes wide with a faint smile tugged at the corner of his lips. Eventually, he turned to Graham. His expression remained one of awe as he extended his hand with unwavering confidence.

"You set up a date. When I say date, I don't mean a hypothetical date. I need a date. Time, location, and the guarantee that she will show up. Once I see proof of this, Herald will take you there."

Graham smiled, extending his arm and shaking hands with Mardian as both maintained eye contact before letting go.

"Well," Mardian said, standing up with a grace that belied his previous fidgeting. He smoothed out the wrinkles in his suit and ran his fingers through his hair, stealing one last glance at Geraldine before turning back to Graham.

"I think it's time Herald and I retire to our rooms. It's been a long day." He placed his hands on Herald's shoulders, gently rousing him from his trance. "We'll continue this conversation tomorrow morning," Mardian said, his voice carrying a note of finality, as he turned and guided his younger brother out of the living room with a confident stride. As the door shut, Graham let his body sink into the couch.

Everything is going perfectly.

He looked to Geraldine once more.

Soon, you'll be mine again…
This time, I won't let you go.

Reverie

Upon opening his eyes, Graham felt his body wrapped tightly in winter's bitter embrace, its frigid coils snaking around him in gentle comfort. At a glance, he noticed a window thrown wide open at the room's end. The pale light of dawn spilt in through it, accompanied by the gentle sound of alpine wind rushing against the hotel's solid facade. Slowly, he got out of bed and began to dress. Having donned a navy-blue shirt and charcoal jeans, he took his place on the bed. She lay motionless, her eyes sealed shut. An overwhelming wave of emotion swept over him as he sat there, staring at her. Gently, he reached out to caress her pallid cheeks, finding himself captivated by all her subtleties. The very essence of her stirred his soul, compelling him to worship her to the core of his being. He *needed* to revere every spec of what was *her*.

Her face
An ivory complexion tinged with paleness,
Flushed rosy cheeks and lips of fiery sweetness.

Her eyes
A delicate network of veins,
barely visible, yet magnetic.

Her hair
Lustrous and vibrant,
dancing to a tune only it could hear.

Her scent
An intoxicating fragrance,
whispering of fields in bloom and honeyed dew.

She was a living,
—breathing—
work of art.

A masterpiece
crafted
by the *divine.*

Every single flaw
she strove
to *erase*
He gave *worship* to.

He had finally reached the point of no return, ready to make his pledge—this time he would not let her go. He took a step back as a dry sensation gripped his mouth, his heart pounding wildly against his chest.

I need to control myself, he thought as he turned to close the window.

Slowly, he crept towards the door and left the room, closing the door behind him. His steps were slow as he made his way down the hallway. In the following moments, he turned left and entered the dining room. A table stood, laden with breakfast foods: cereals, baked goods, scrambled eggs, bacon, yoghurt, and fruits. Caroline and Herald were already seated in the left-end corner of the room. Caroline drank what appeared to be chamomile tea, accompanied by a croissant adorned with butter and a spread of strawberry jam on her plate. Herald sat with a cluttered bowl of fruits and cereal, seemingly untouched. While walking up to the buffet, Herald peered at Graham with an incredulous look. Indifferent to it, Graham grabbed a mug and headed toward the coffee machine that stood in the corner.

Coffee — black.

Amid the slow filling of his mug, he noticed the two midgets entering the room. They were deep in conversation, eagerly debating with one another. Stumbling over to the buffet table, they were unaware of Graham's presence. As Graham turned to head towards an empty table, Herbert bumped into him, causing them both to lose their balance.

"Graham! I'm so sorry. I didn't see you there," Herbert remarked.

"I want to finalise our plans," Graham replied.

"Yes, of course. Find a place to sit. We'll uh-we'll be right there."

What an absolute idiot, Graham thought as he gradually made his way to the table at the entrance of the room, a considerable distance from Herald and Caroline. He sat down, catching Herald's sharp gaze from the other end of the room. Caroline had already eaten her food, leaving behind a pristine, clean. Her hands were clasped around Herald's fingers, whispering incessantly in his ear. Taking a sip of coffee, Graham turned his attention away from them. Mardian and Herbert were already making their way towards him, carrying an array of plates, each fully stocked with enough food to feed a family of ten. Sitting across from him, Herbert chowed down on his plate of eggs, grits, and bacon with the same enthrallment as a pig who had been without food. Meanwhile, Mardian left his food unattended and sat across from Graham with his hands held tightly in front of him, a burning intensity in his eyes.

"Have you spoken to her?" Mardian asked, his voice insistent.

"Yes, she's not available till tomorrow," Graham affirmed.

"Where's your proof?" Mardian's brows furrowed.

A smug look spread across Graham's face as he reached into his pocket and retrieved a slim sterling necklace. A subtle blush swept over Mardian's face, his eyes widening as Graham held it up. At its bottom, a diamond flickered, its twinkle visible in Mardian's gaze. He coughed, drawing Mardian's attention to him. Graham's hands rapidly closed around the necklace, concealing it within his grasp.

"I want your brother to take me there now."

Graham declared, maintaining a fixed sight on Mardian.

"Now? It's too dangerous, the snow still hasn't cleared." Mardian said, retiring into his chair.

"I'm not flexible on this," Graham replied.

A drop of sweat trickled down Mardian's forehead as he gazed at Herbert who was feverishly slurping coffee and gnawing on chocolate croissants. Readjusting his tie and hair, Mardian turned back to Graham. He fixed his gaze on Graham, his fingers lightly tapping the table's edge. Re-adjusting his posture in the chair, Mardian spoke, "Fine. But I want my brother brought back safe and alive. If he's not back in one piece you and I will have serious issues, and this woman will pay the price."

With the same conviction on his face, Graham extended his hand towards Mardian. In a slow and deliberate manner, he let the supple necklace fall into the man's plump palms. The delicate object slipped from his grasp as Mardian feverishly shoved it into the breast pocket of his charcoal blazer. Tapping his brother's shoulder, Mardian startled Herbert, resulting in him dropping the spoon from which he was savouring his rice pudding.

"We meet at 7:00 by the entrance. Don't be late," Mardian said as he joined his brother in standing.

In a matter of seconds, they both departed from the dining room. Herbert's side of the table was piled high with dingy plates and soggy drinks, while Mardian had not even touched his breakfast. It was only when Graham glanced towards the end of the room that he realised Caroline and Herald too had left. Standing up, Graham approached their table. An opulent ebony-black business card framed in gold adorned Herald's side of the table. With a quick grasp of the item, Graham tucked it into his pocket and sauntered out of the room. His swift ascent of the stairs led him to the second floor, where he sought room 212. Slowly making his way, he suddenly felt a tingling sensation of being watched. Progressing down the hallway, his footsteps gradually fell silent. Suddenly, an unexpected hand seized him from the side, pulling him into a tight corner of the hallway. Herald's plump hands clutched his neck, his once-lucid blue eyes now blazing with a fiery red hue. Herald tightened his grip, his fingernails slowly carving into Graham's skin. The air around them grew thick and suffocating.

"I know what you've done," Herald hissed, spitting on Graham, who was already struggling to breathe from the pungent odour of Herald's breath, his decaying teeth inches from Graham's face.

"I don't know what you're talking about," Graham said, steadily fighting for air.

"My wife saw you enter yesterday. Room 212, am I right?" A growing sense of frustration filled Herald's voice, as his grip tightened.

A smile drew across Graham's face as he actively maintained eye contact with Herald. He felt the grip tighten even further as the nails biting into his neck drew blood.

"I wouldn't be so quick with accusations," Graham spoke, barely audible. In his pocket, he retrieved the black card he had found before, holding it up to Herald's eye level. Herald's grip remained firm, seemingly unaffected by the item.

"Admit to what you've done sicko before I have you killed."

The smile on Graham's face remained, as spoke,

"You're not Herald, are you?" Graham snorted.

35

Herald tightened his grip until Graham's breath was cut short. Struggling to speak, he choked out a whimper, his body wracked with spasms. As his vision dimmed, he fought with every ounce of strength he had left, his gasps for air growing more desperate. The world around him faded into obscurity, a single thought echoing in his mind.

Geraldine—Geraldine—Geral—Geral—ldine—ldine—dine—dine—die—diedied.

Ignis Fatuus

With a single glance, the world slowly returned to Graham's sight as he opened his eyes. He lay sprawled on the ground, a bulky pair of charcoal boots inches from his face. His eyes caught the sight of Herald engaged in a heated discussion with Caroline. Still struggling to gather his bearings, he heard their voices, incessant and distorted. Remaining as stout and passive as possible, he hoped they would not become aware of his waking state.

"Herald, we need to let this go. He knows."

Caroline said in a hurry, clutching Herald's arm with increasing vigour. Flames of fury still blazed in Herald's eyes.

"I can't let him do this."

He said, his gaze fixed on Caroline's. "I need to put an end to it."

Upon pleading again, Caroline's eyes began to water.

"Think of Mia. They'll come after her. Herald. They will take her. You know they will."

Tears soon poured down Herald's cheeks, his fiery crimson eyes still holding the same hue. After a moment of silence, he spoke, "We need to leave before I change my mind."

"Of course, let's go. Let's pack up and leave."

Caroline sighed, gently wiping away the tears that had begun to trickle down his face. Looking up, she caught his gaze, she smiled, and so did he.

"We have to go," she said.

"I know," he replied.

She embraced him tightly, holding him close. Both sighed, briefly staying in place.

"We'll make it through this," she mumbled, her words a silent promise of hope. Breaking from the embrace, she looked at him once more.

"Let's go," she said, turning around, swiftly making her way down the hall. He followed her, a few steps behind. Only halfway through the corridor did she realise how quiet it had become. All that could be heard were her footsteps.

"Herald?"

As she turned back, a sudden rush of adrenaline ran through her body.

"Herald!"

Further down the hallway, he stood still, a knife buried deep in his chest. Her heart sank and a wave of nausea overtook her. In a moment of paralysis, fear gripped her lungs. Without a second thought, she ran towards him. It was not long before blood began to drain from his body. She could feel the slow dragging beat of her heart as she ran, hoping to fool the passage of time. Her heart skipped a beat as his body gradually slid down the wall, followed by a resounding, concussive thump to the ground.

"HERALD!" she shrieked at the top of her lungs; her eyes filled with hysteria.

Throwing herself on the floor beside him, she looked at the knife in a state of panic. She went into shock, amazed at the amount of blood his body held. In desperately looking up at him, she realised that his face had turned pale and empty, his eyes back to the same hue of blue they had held before.

"Herald what happened! What do I do? I-I don't know what to do—"

A flood of tears welled up in her eyes, obscuring her vision as she spoke in haste. Trying to stop the bleeding, she tore off her shirt frantically, trying to apply enough pressure to the wound with her now numb and crippled hands. With her stomach churning, she squeezed the shirt tight around the wound as blood relentlessly gushed down her bare arms. She exerted all her energy, her heart rate skyrocketing. At the top of her lungs, she screamed, "HEL—"

Herald's hands muffled her voice. She looked up into his eyes, attempting to scream once more, but his grip remained firm.

"Take Mia," he said.

She shook her head frantically, tears and snot streaming down her cheeks as she felt pain roar throughout her body.

"Take Mia, and leave."

Unwilling to accept it, she shoved her shirt into his chest, burying it as deeply as she possibly could. He tore the soaked fabric from her hands, throwing it across the room. Blood rushed out at a rapid rate.

"Go. Now!"

She felt her heart buckle as her body grew numb, a sense of realisation forming within her. Slowly, his tight grip began to weaken, until he could no longer hold his hands up. Her heart pounded in her chest as she watched his eyes slowly close. A deep realisation struck her in sharp waves of pain.

The hallway suddenly rang with a quiet, high-pitched voice.

"Mom?"

A wave of dread crept over Caroline as she turned to the hallway, her stomach churning. "Mia!" she said, rapidly shifting her body to the side, trying to cover up Herald. Frozen in place, Mia stood, her favourite plush rabbit in hand.

"What's going on? Why is Haldi on the floor?"

Tears in her eyes, Caroline was lost at what to say.

"He's just resting for a moment. Go-go back to your room and pack your bags. We will be there soon, Haldi just needs to rest for a bit," Caroline said softly, concealing the tremble in her voice. Despite this, Mia remained still, not moving, her eyes frantically flicking between Herald and Caroline in a search for something.

"Mia, go," Caroline said.

Shrugging her shoulders, Mia turned to leave.

"Mia—" Herald suddenly spoke. Bringing her to a complete halt. "Haldi?" she said looking back.

A smile spread across his face as he spoke once more.

"I love you. Don't ever forget that" he said.

"I love you too Haldi!" Mia exclaimed, smiling, trying to keep her balance as she skidded out of the hallway toward the stairs.

Another phase of dread filled Caroline as she turned to Herald only to find his eyes locked shut. She desperately sought a pulse but could only find a crushing silence. Amidst a frozen state, her shoulders slumped under the weight of death's hands. Tears, swollen and saturated with grief, flowed thick and fast from her eyes. The deep realisation washed over her, crashing against the shores of her consciousness in sharp, relentless waves of pain. Her hands clenched tightly onto his, desperate to hold on to a fading connection. With each painful breath that caught her throat, she felt herself choking on grief's bitter taste. The hall embraced a heavy silence, punctuated only by shallow breaths, the relentless pounding of her heart, and silent cries of sorrow. Lost in the quiet solitude of the hallway, Caroline found herself consumed by memories and the weight of her grief. The silence enveloped her like an oppressive shroud, broken only by the distant howling wind that fiercely kissed the hotel's unyielding facade.

Yet, within that stillness, a sound shattered her trance. At first, a mere whisper, it gradually swelled, echoing through the desolate corridors. Caroline's ears perked up, her heart leaping in its chest, sensing the presence of something unsettling. Footsteps. Distinct and deliberate, they seemed to draw closer, each step infused with an unwelcome purpose. With each passing moment, they drew nearer, their echo reverberating through the hallway, sending a shiver coursing through her veins. Her trembling hand reached out, fingertips brushing against Herald's cheek in a bittersweet caress, as if etching the memory of their love into her very being. Nearing him, she leaned in, her voice a soft caress, as tears gracefully streamed down her cheeks.

"When the time is right, we will meet again. Right now, our story has come to a close, its pages filled, but in another distant realm, a new chapter awaits to be written. Wherever you have gone, please don't forget me. Wait for me like I'll wait for you. Wait for us. For our forever. *I love you.*"

With a heavy heart, she turned away, her steps heavy with the burden of her sorrow. Time pressed upon her, urging her to seek refuge. Her steps faltered along the dimly lit corridor, each creaking floorboard resonating through her soul. She arrived at the door of room 212, a place she had subconsciously avoided, sensing an ever-present, foreboding presence lurking within. Summoning every ounce of courage, she swallowed her fear; her trembling hand pushing the door open, granting her passage into the room. The air inside hung heavy, tainted with the pervasive scent of decay and a bone-chilling cold. Moonlight, a ghostly spectre, filtered through time-stained windows, its ethereal touch casting dancing shadows upon faded wallpaper. As she stepped into the room, her gaze swept across the dimly lit space, her eyes adjusting to the ambience. Her heart skipped a beat as she noticed a figure resting on the bed, lying in peaceful slumber. Her form exuded an air of tranquillity, her features softened in the embrace of blissful sleep, cocooned in a serene state, oblivious to her surroundings. The moonlight's gentle caress painted a delicate glow upon her slumbering form, casting an ethereal radiance that contrasted with the room's sombre atmosphere.

Who are you? Caroline thought.

Eudaemonia

Taking refuge in the electrical closet by the stairway, Graham stood still, struggling to contain his breath. A sense of compulsion obliged him to remain silent and unnoticed. As if in a state of trance, he stood motionless, nothing more than his laboured breathing marking his presence. Despite his best efforts, he could not make sense of what had transpired in a matter of what had felt like seconds. Only a vague memory remained of Herald looming over him, his posture having changed. It was as if time itself had skipped a page. As if his memory had forgotten to consider the events that were to follow. In the short period following that moment, he only remembered finding himself in the closet, his hands shaking incessantly and the hall erupting with shrieks of distress. Amid his confusion and panic, he remained in place. Suddenly, the hallway filled with the echoed voice of a girl as she dashed down the stairs. In his state of haze, Graham could not make sense of her words. A cloud of disorientation filled his world once more, causing gravity to bear down on his feet. It was then that the girl abruptly skipped to the stairway before slowly ascending it. A faint and inconsistent sound could be heard as she climbed the stairwell. Sometimes stopping completely, leaving an unsettling lull in her wake. In an effort to calm his breathing, he closed his eyes, trying to recall the circumstances leading up to this point. But the more he deliberated, the fainter the memory became. Slowly, he opened his eyes, discovering the girl's footsteps had ceased altogether. In the darkness, he was left alone, only a faint whisper of her presence. Taking a deep breath, he prepared to leave. Emerging from the closet, motion sensors in the hallway triggered the stairwell light to illuminate. He needed to find Herbert. He needed to do it—for *her*.

For Geraldine…

As he turned to proceed down the stairs, he heard another set of footsteps. Struggling to discern them, his heartbeat quickened once more. A faint heaviness and lag characterised the movement as if someone was dragging their feet across the floor. Minute after minute, the footsteps grew in proximity. Having no desire to take any chances, he discreetly returned to the closet, closing its doors gently. Through its opening, he observed a diminutive figure standing. It was Margareta, proceeding up the stairs. Following her figure, it became apparent that she carried a handgun. On reaching his floor, she stepped past the closet, following the screams down the hallway, weapon in hand. Having opened the closet door quietly, Graham ascended the staircase so as not to be heard. Following his entry into the hallway, he proceeded towards the front door. Retrieving his coat from the corner of the entrance room, he swiftly adorned it.

Time was of the essence.

Briskly, he buttoned up his coat and turned to leave. Taking a deep breath, he stood still for a moment's time, trying to maintain his composure. As he swung the door open, an icy gust of wind whipped him across the face, temporarily obstructing his vision. Adjusting quickly to the surrounding light, away from the darkness that pervaded the hotel, he turned to see Herbert standing in front of him. He had dressed in nothing more than a slender suit and gauze that virtually disguised his appearance in its entirety. Upon seeing Graham, he exhibited no response. Slowly approaching one another, neither spoke a word.

Furrowing his brow, Herbert spoke, "Where were you?"

"Minor complications," Graham replied.

Gritting his teeth, Herbert turned and proceeded to a path within the woodland. Graham followed him down the winding path, his heart racing with anticipation. As they delved deeper into the woods, a dense sea of fog descended upon them. The air grew stagnant, its suffocating nature making it ideal for those who flourished in the dark, worshipping its negligence. Branches of skinny, old, decaying trees hung with dense moss, making passage more difficult as they clustered together. Grassy rocks embedded in the ground were dotted with moss, spiderwebs trailing along with its shadows, where spiders waited patiently—yearning for the chance to feast on bloated bodies and hot blood. A hushed silence filled the landscape, interrupted only by the rustling of weed between their trousers. A fog had moved into the forest floor, covering it in a veil of poltergeist-white mist. Through its spineless tentacles, it distorted the shape of nature. A distant buzz rang in the woods to the north.

We're close.

Herbert walked closely ahead, grouching and huffing at every step. Graham tightened his coat around him. The cold had already penetrated past his coat, through his skin and right to his core. His entire body ached with tension as he struggled against the cold, his neck aching as a result of the strain. A thick fog of breath gathered in his mouth as he attempted to retain warmth, causing an icy chill to linger in his mouth. No matter how tightly he pulled his coat around him, the frigid air still seeped in. Aware that he was unable to conserve any further heat, he focused his efforts on completing the task at hand.

A raspy utterance suddenly escaped Herbert's lips, "We're here."

In only his suit and scarf, he appeared impervious to the bitterness of winter's kiss. Looking up from his shoes, Graham was met by an awe-inspiring landscape. He gazed at the shimmering waters of a lake that lay down below, cradled by snow-capped mountains. Transfixed, he gazed at the sun's reflection as it set. With its ethereal hues, the setting sun gave him the feeling that he was standing in a paradise that time had long forgotten. On the vast hilltop lay an open expanse, stretching out flat as far as the eye could see. At its pinnacle loomed a colossal edifice with a deep well at its centre, casting a shadow over the surrounding trees and vegetation. A state of complete reverence prevailed over Graham. For once, he was not bigger than life.

Herbert had already made his way towards the marble stairway that led to the well. While all else was encrusted with grime and debris, the structure itself was meticulously clean. Not a single scratch, smudge, or blemish present. As if polished and preserved with an acute attention to detail, the marble steps emitted a luminescence distinctive of its surroundings.

"Are you coming or not?" Herbert asked, his voice tinged with irritation.

Taking his time, Graham continued up the steps towards the well. In reaching into the lower pocket of his jacket, his hands, frozen to the point of skeletal immobility, had difficulty grasping the object. He felt as his fingertips brushed against the delicate silver thread, also encased by winter's grasp. Then, reaching in, he tangled it around his fingertips, tightly clutching it. On reaching the top of the structure, he peered down the well, revealing a vast, seemingly endless void. The longer he stood looking at it, the more he felt himself about to fall. His other hand dug into his pocket, retrieving a picture he always carried. Looking at it, a flood of tears filled his eyes. There she was, encircled by his arms, both beaming with happiness. In a moment of realisation, he was beset by an intense sense of loss. Withholding tears, his fingers traced her silhouette as he recalled their time together. Inhaling deeply, his gaze remained fixed on her, absorbing memories of the past

...Geraldine...
She left but she never truly—*left.*

...Geraldine...
The t r a i l of her once present love,
forever cemented in his mind,
forever imprinting his heart.

...Geraldine...
A past consistently thought,
but never spoken of.

...Geraldine...
A chapter he refused to recite.

...Geraldine...
And like the moon
He arose each night,
some days fuller than others,
seeking out her dying light.

...Geraldine...
He searched for her in the stars.
In every sunrise,
and every sun fall.

...Geraldine...
Trapped in between
wanting to forget,
and
wanting to hold on.

...Geraldine...
There was no noise greater,
than the silence of two people
—once lovers
The unsaid loudly echoed in the silent void.

...Geraldine...
An interconnected, submerged aching.
A shared feeling of regret.

...Geraldine...

A story left unfinished,

but its chapters long closed.

Do you remember?

I know I do.

I remember.

You know that don't you?

Remind me

The reason of our departure

That which tore us apart

I can fix it...

But how can I fix a thing

Once broken but now gone?

I'm afraid

I'll miss you forever.

I need you

I hope one day — you'll need me too.

I hope one day we'll need each other.

Reunited

...Never to be forgotten...

With that, he took out the necklace he had been holding
onto the entire time. *Geraldine's* necklace. He raised his hand
above the well as the gleaming pearl dangled from above. His
memory of her suddenly collapsed, shattered by a sharp,
sweltering pain piercing him from behind. A wave of paralysis
swept across his legs, leaving him in a state of staggered
disorientation. As he searched for the source, a deep red
blotch began to form across his shirt, seeping into his jacket.

Unable to move, his body collapsed as he fell down the stairs, every crack and fissure piercing his body as he fell. In the instant following his halt, his body grew cold as he turned his gaze toward the now-murky sky. A delicate snowfall began to fall, coating his body. As the snow settled on his skin, a chill swept through him. Soon after, a hand grasped his shoulder, accompanied by an echoed utterance. He made an attempt to speak, but none of his words came out. Herbert stood, hovering over him, a sinister grin spreading across his face. He tightened his grip around Graham's shoulder, a chill penetrating further into his body. Herbert spoke, his voice an amalgam of a whisper and a hiss. There was an air of levity about his words, almost tangible. In what was evolving into a blizzard, Graham felt the cold slipping through his clothes. Amid the looming presence of Herbert, his breath congealed in his throat. He found himself unable to move or speak. All he could do was observe, as Herbert slowly made his way around Graham's body. Snorting and puffing, he eagerly took Graham's hand and snatched the necklace. Graham tried to resist, but found himself rooted in place, unable to do more than watch as Herbert took the necklace—as he took *her.* Slowly Herbert made his way up the stairs, breathless, his footsteps slow, erratic, and heavy.

No...

Once atop the structure, without a moment's hesitation, Herbert tossed the necklace into the abyss. Soon after, a deep splash echoed across the landscape, announcing its descent into the murky waters below. The ground shook as a portion of the ornamental lines that encircled the statue flickered to life. Herbert took out a knife and plunged it into his palm, cascading his blood into the abyss. With a satiated look, he stepped away from the well and stood back as the line of light illuminated the entire site. He had made a deal with a force greater than himself, and it had been fulfilled. The ground began shifting once more, this time more violently, as the rest of the ornamental lines lit up. A bright light emanated from the well before everything dwindled into complete darkness, obliterating light from both the structure and the surrounding atmosphere. All that remained was winter's bitter embrace. He had done it. He had successfully negotiated with the gods, and his reward was coming to fruition. The tremors that enveloped the land were the heralds of an emerging and formidable entity, one that no one could deny. At once, a wind began howling in the far distance, alongside a high-pitched whistle. In steady progression, it grew in proximity and intensified. A heavy gust of wind blasted through the atmosphere, thrusting Graham deeper into the ground, leaving the midget to tumble and fall flat on the surface. Suddenly the sun emerged, but it didn't light up the rest of the atmosphere. It hovered in solitude, an ethereal crystalline circle in a vacuum of darkness. The ground shook once more. In the wake of another severe gust of wind, a bright white light consumed the earth.

Fatalis

An unsettling aura hung in the air, consuming Caroline's senses. As she fixed her gaze on the window, a sudden sense of surveillance washed over her. A sliver of light, delicate and fragile, breached the confines of heavy drapes, teasing her with glimpses of the outside world. She caught a glimpse of a raven that sat on the windowsill, its gaze fixed upon her. They looked into each other's eyes, sorrow and pity dominating their minds. In an instant, the raven broke their trance before taking flight. In the muted stillness it left behind, a gentle breath of wind stirred, coaxing the window open with a subtle creak, bringing with it a wintry breath that brushed against Caroline's face. In an instant, the wind transformed into a gale as the window swung wide open, relinquishing a tenuous hold on the room. Snowflakes, delicate and crystalline, twirled and pirouetted, creating a mesmerising ballet as an ethereal beauty danced in the midst of chaos.

With an explosive climax, the wind washed over the hotel, roaring and shrieking with a piercing intensity. Caroline clung desperately to the nearby bed frame, feeling the reverberations of the growing storm rattle her very being. Suddenly, a blinding light descended upon the room, ensnaring her within its radiant grasp. Weightless and suspended in time and space, Caroline found herself engulfed by the blinding light, overwhelming her senses with its celestial glow. The world around her faded into oblivion as if devoured by its luminous jaws. She fell, collapsing onto the unyielding floor, tumbling through the room on her hands and knees, losing herself within a chaotic interplay of light and darkness.

Eventually, the luminescence gradually receded, and Caroline regained her footing, her bewildered eyes adjusting to the transformed world outside the window. The once-familiar landscape was now obscured by an inky darkness that smothered the surroundings, suffocating the remnants of the world. Yet, the sun persevered—a radiant orb blazing against the darkness. Its light, unable to pierce the dark void that had consumed everything in its path. Caroline turned her gaze inward, her eyes drawn to the bed where the girl had lain moments ago. Time unfurled before her eyes, as the bed suddenly began to swallow within itself into a growing abyss. As the vast hole expanded relentlessly, Caroline's outstretched hand quivered with desperation, yearning to grasp hold of the girl. But before her fingertips could brush even the faintest trace of her, the figure was swiftly engulfed by the abyss. The void began devouring the room, its yawning maw consuming everything in its path. Transfixed by a maelstrom of grief and terror, Caroline fled the room, her heart hammering in her chest. With trembling urgency, she swung open the door, her gaze confronted with a gun aimed directly at her face, wielded by Margareta. Caroline's frantic words faltered, silenced by a single, piercing sound as Margareta pulled the trigger.

Hiraeth

Trees—Bound to the earthly plane
Assailed by the winds' fury
Fated to expire
But always,
Present

Snow—
A symphony of ice and air
Each flake cold and tender
Melding in a wintry affair
Destined to converge and surrender
But always,
Present

The sun—
A celestial traveller
Embracing all beneath its golden touch
Until its withdrawal
Yielding to the nocturnal embrace
But always,
Present

The wind—
In rhythmic flow
It dances
Circumnavigating all
In nature's waltz.
Sometimes intense
In moments of fervent might,
Yet also gentle
A touch as soft as moonlight
But always,
Present

Love—
A puzzle undefined
A symphony of shifting tides
A will that remains its own
Sometimes intense
Like thunderous storms
Other times silent
With secrets only weary hearts know
But always,
Present

Desire—
A flame
Poised to ignite
At times embraced
a quest of passion ablaze
Other times concealed
Hidden from sight
But always,

Present

Geraldine—
Once his bliss
Now his pain
But always,
Present

Geraldine—
An alluring obsession
Weaving his tale
Bound against his logical mind
Nevertheless
Always Present

Geraldine—
The cornerstone
The narrative's spine
Or a mere catalyst, defining his course?
Nevertheless
Always Present

Geraldine—In every word
Every chapter
Every action
Every space
Always Present

Geraldine
Always Present

Present

Burn
Burn
Burn
Burn
Burn
Burn
Burn

And there he was once more. At the threshold of the hotel's footsteps.

Like a cycle—he would arrive, disappear, and return—a broken circuit.

"Am I ready?"

Hesitation arose once more. As if it had never left. A constant presence. Now, however, his perspective had changed. *Desire* had become a festering wound, steering the ship, while *Reality* and *Consciousness* looked on from the sidelines. With a newfound fervour, he pressed forward, embracing the power *it* had granted him.

"Yes, I am."

A sudden force struck him from within, driving him to grasp at the door handle. No longer wishing to rely on someone else to grant admission, he chose to act on his own behalf. And yet, the further he reached, the further he seemed to be from it. In confusion, he glanced upward.

It was—gone. Not a trace present.

Looking up, he found nothing. He was ready, but the opportunity had passed. Beyond the top of the steps lay the vast landscape of the Austrian Alps. Originally a hotel, now a deep *Abyss* in its place. In a flash, his vision dimmed as he grasped for his stomach. It had completely slipped his mind— he was dying—bleeding out.

The clock was ticking. He needed to act.

Geraldine…

For all these years, he had been too afraid to speak. He had resisted. *Opportunity* stood right before his eyes, and he chose to neglect it. Afraid of the unknown, he followed in *Fear's* lead. It had been his barrier, deterring him from pursuing opportunities and assuming risks. Even when he had the opportunity to make the change, *Fear* inhibited him and kept him from fulfilling his potential. *Fear* had kept him apart…apart from *her*.

"GERALDINE!" he bellowed, his voice echoing through the vast hole.

His throat trembled as tears slowly filled his eyes. Grief-stricken, he repeatedly cried out her name, determined to keep her memory alive. His voice faltered, yet he persisted in his pleas—a testament to *Desire*. As his heart slowly crumbled, the only pain he felt penetrated deep into his inner being. If only he had possessed the courage he now commands. If only he had the ability to turn back time. If only he could tell her how he truly felt.

If only—If only—
"GERALDINE!"

Slowly, his voice began to give out. A growing darkness engulfed the world, drawing him closer and closer to the *Abyss*. His voice quivered in fear as he inched closer to the edge, knowing full well the danger that lay ahead. He begged time to turn back. He begged for another chance. He begged *Fate* to allow him to reconsider.

"GERALDINE!"
It was too late—he knew it.

"GERALDINE!"
He needed to let her go.

"GERALDINE!"
Holding onto her was like grasping at a handful of water.

"GERALDINE!"
No matter how hard he tried.

"GERALDINE!"
It was inevitable she would slip through his fingers.

"GERALDINE!"
She was never his to keep,

"GERALDINE!"
Never his to hold.

"GERALDINE!"

Close enough to see,

"GERALDINE!"

But too far to reach.

Gradually, he approached the *Abyss*. It was the end—his end. He had failed, and life was ready to take him. With a deep breath, he accepted his fate; a fate that he had sealed with his own hands. He stepped into the vast hole without a second's delay. Gradually, his body let go as he relinquished his control to Life.

In a way, it felt comforting. Finally, he was able to flow in the rhythm of life's stream. Finally, he was able to become a part of nature. With a final sigh, he accepted his place in the world, content with the knowledge that he was now a part of something bigger than himself. In his calm state, he almost felt as if he were floating. Liberated and connected, as if the universe was embracing him with a warm hug. As he reflected once more, he was only left with one thought.

Geraldine…Geraldine…Geraldine…Geraldine…Geraldine…Geraldine…Geraldine…Geraldine…

"Is there anything that has been bothering you?"

It plagued her mind, just as it did his. Despite all the words that had been left unspoken, their silence spoke of a truth they had both chosen to omit.

Logic told them it was mutual, but *Fear* drove them to reconsider.

"I've just been thinking about ~~you~~ a lot of things, and I'm not sure If I understand my own thoughts yet."

If only they had taken a chance. If only they followed their heart. If only they dared to dream. For months, they had been afraid of taking *Chance* by its hand. For months, they had convinced themselves against it. For months, they had thought that confiding in *Ignorance* would make it go away. Yet, over time, their longing continued to fester itself within, sinking deeper and deeper—an ever-escalating descent, forever plaguing their minds.

Only if they knew—the regret borne by *Inaction* far outweighed the risk assumed by *Action*.

"But…you know I'm here for you, right? You don't need to be scared to talk to me. I promise I would never judge you. I'm here for you, and nobody else…It's just that, I can tell something has been bothering you, and I don't want to be intrusive, I just want to let you know that ~~I can't get you out of my head~~ whatever you need, I'm here."

Here they sat, just beyond the threshold of a decision. In facing one another, they held *Aspiration* the same way they held *Reluctance*. As a distant observer, *Decision* patiently awaited the verdict, while *Stillness* hovered in the room with the clock blinking unobtrusively. They sat across from each other, a coffee table in separation, accompanied by three other decision makers who had not been seen but were present nevertheless. *Fear—Rationale—Sentiment.*

"It's just that…~~I can't get you out of my head too~~ I hate that I am so capable of speaking the truth when advising others, but when it comes to myself, I am somehow always incapable of following my own advice."

Sentiment stepped in, prompting him towards *Action*. And yet, *Fear* overpowered, pushing him towards *Stillness*. He looked up at her once more, *Sentiment* weighing heavily on his shoulders, churning and twisting his inner gut—it was what kept him up at night, constantly weighing him down, overwhelming his mind and racing his heart. Suddenly, *Rationality* interjected, shoving *Fear* aside, forcing his mouth open as he suddenly found himself speaking.

"I need to ask you something."

She looked up at him, as their eyes met, *Sentiment* drawing them closer together. Their eyes held the same glow of affection and tenderness, woven with a thread of regret. Why couldn't they just go for it? They both knew on a deeper level that they shared the same *Sentiment*. But *Subconscious* held them back from *Action*, compelling them to confide in *Fear*—masquerading as *Rationality*. The two locked eyes, their hearts aflame with the same ardour. They could feel *Desire* urging them together, but *Hesitation* stood firmly in between—like a mighty river caught in a dam, desperate to cascade, yet held back by the shackles of *Uncertainty*.

"Is there something you're holding back?"

He asked, his eyes focused straight on hers. They both knew what question he was asking, and what response he was hoping for. She wanted to say it. Her heart ached to scream it with all its might, but instead, she opted to confide in *Fear*.

"~~Yes, there is~~ No, I don't think so."

Silence swept the room, as *Desire* grew in size—its presence more and more tangible.

"Do you?"

She asked, scrutinising his face once more, pleading in her mind that he would confide in *Sentiment* unlike her. His gaze was fixed on hers. All he wanted was her. And he knew deep down that she shared that longing. He struggled against himself, as *Fear*, *Rationale* and *Sentiment* argued feverishly against one another. His gaze fell to the ground as he broke eye contact—every cell in his body yearned for it, every fibre of his being begged for it, every inch of his soul ached for it. Throughout the room, he searched and pleaded for *Courage*. Suddenly, he noticed it. Lurking in the corner of the room—untouched. In a plea for help, he called out to it. It looked up at him, and suddenly *Hope* walked over and grabbed *Courage* by the hand, gently guiding it.

This time, he thought, *I won't hold back.*

Finally, he could explore a reality he had been dreaming of his. He looked back at her, *Courage* and *Hope* now present, holding him by the hands.

"Geraldine," he spoke softly, his heart beating feverishly.

"Yes?" she said, looking into his eyes, her heart brimming for the words she had been yearning to hear come from his mouth.

Slowly, he opened his mouth to speak once more, "I—"

Decision stood up in his seat, eagerly waiting for him to speak once more.

"I—"

"~~I love you~~ I'm just worried about you. That's all."

And just like that, *Hope* and *Courage* were gone once more, now mere distant observers, as *Fear* stood proudly once more—hands resting on his shoulders.

Despite wanting to believe that this was the blame for his fate. He knew deep down who the real catalyst was—He was travelling right through it.

—Desire—

A bottomless pit
An *Abyss* at its heart
Enthralled with infinite cravings
With no satisfaction to suffice its longings
Not formed by man
Rather born from within
Man—its vessel
Extorted day by day
By a force that grips
Yet never rescinds
Until he himself
Reaches an inevitable end

Desire
Always Present.